OPEN

OPEN

OPEN

TO BE

AWAKE

To David, Bodhi, and Ryder, my tiny universe

Published by Roaring Brook Press • Roaring Brook Press is a division of Holtzbrinck Publishing Holdings Limited Partnership • 120 Broadway, New York, NY 10271 • mackids.com • Copyright © 2021 by Mags DeRoma

 Library of Congress Control Number 2020924213 • ISBN 978–1–250–7531–9-9 • Our books may be purchased in bulk for promotional, educational, or business use. Please contact your local bookseller or the Macmillan Corporate and Premium Sales Department at (800) 221–7945 ext. 5442 or by email at MacmillanSpecialMarkets@macmillan.com. • First edition, 2021 • Book design by Mercedes Padró • The art for this book was made with paint and soft pastels on a gazillion pieces of cut paper, all collaged together. Printed in China by RR Donnelley Asia Printing Solutions Ltd., Dongguan City, Guangdong Province • 10 9 8 7 6 5 4 3 2 1

AWAKE

MAGS DeROMA

Roaring Brook Press
New York

In a big, big city, on a busy city street, there is a pretty tall
building. At the tipity-top of that tall building is my bedroom.

NEWS

ARTISTS'
GALLERIES
UP STAIRS

One night,
   after a story, a snuggle,
   and one last sip of water,
      Oscar and I were getting SO SLEEPY . . .

when out of the corner of my eye . . .

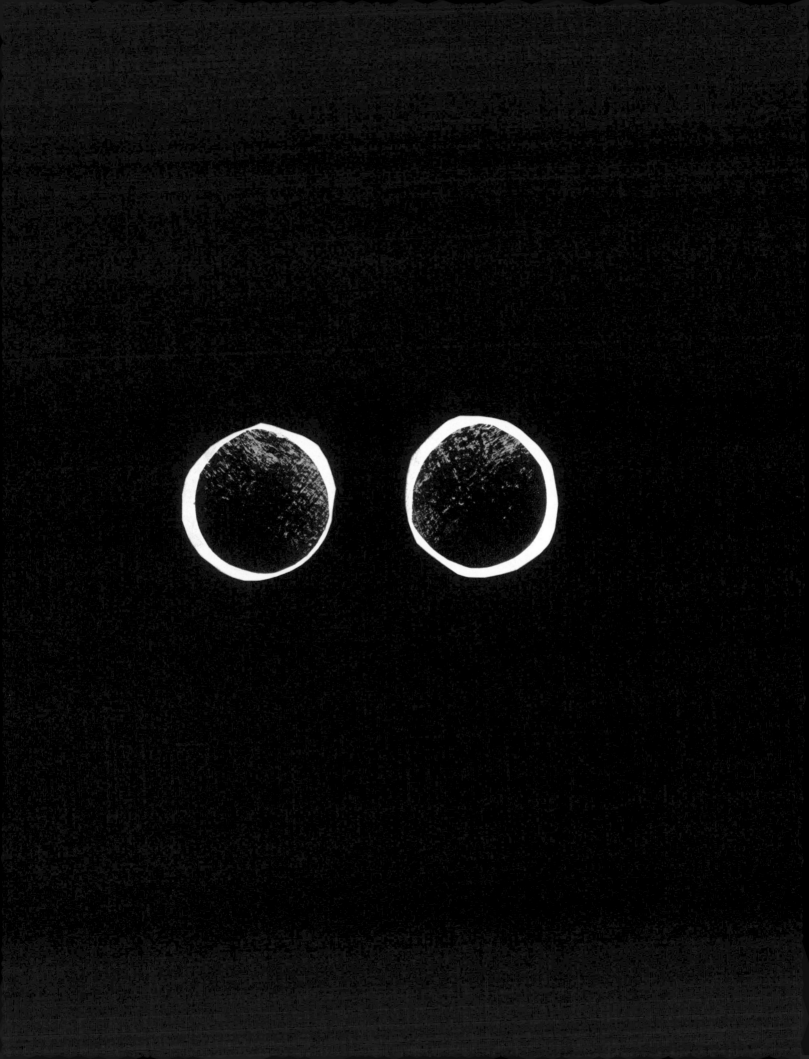

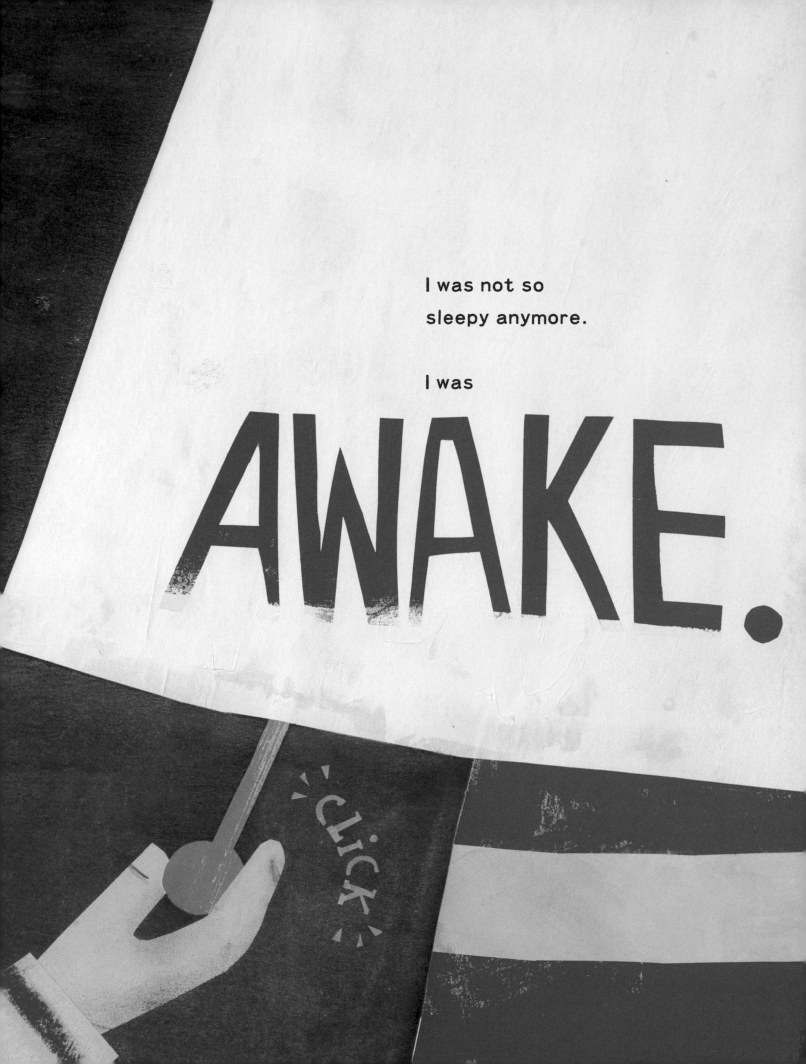

I was not so
sleepy anymore.

I was

AWAKE.

click

NO WAY was I
going to sleep with
a SPIDER in my room.

I looked up
  and down
and all around
     for something
     to smash it with . . .

but there was nothing suitable in sight.

Maybe
if I shut my eyes,
it would leave.

Go away,
HAIRY BEAST!

BAH!
Still there.

I know! The WATER SPOUT!
Just like the RAIN,
I'll WASH the spider out!

But
then out comes
the sun . . .

and dries up
all the rain . . .

and that big hairy
spider CANNOT come
up the spout again,
thank you very much!

I was NOT giving up, though—no way.
I thought of more ideas.
Loads and loads of them.

OH DEAR

I had to think bigger.
WAY bigger.

Maybe,
with some brain power
and an inner tube . . .

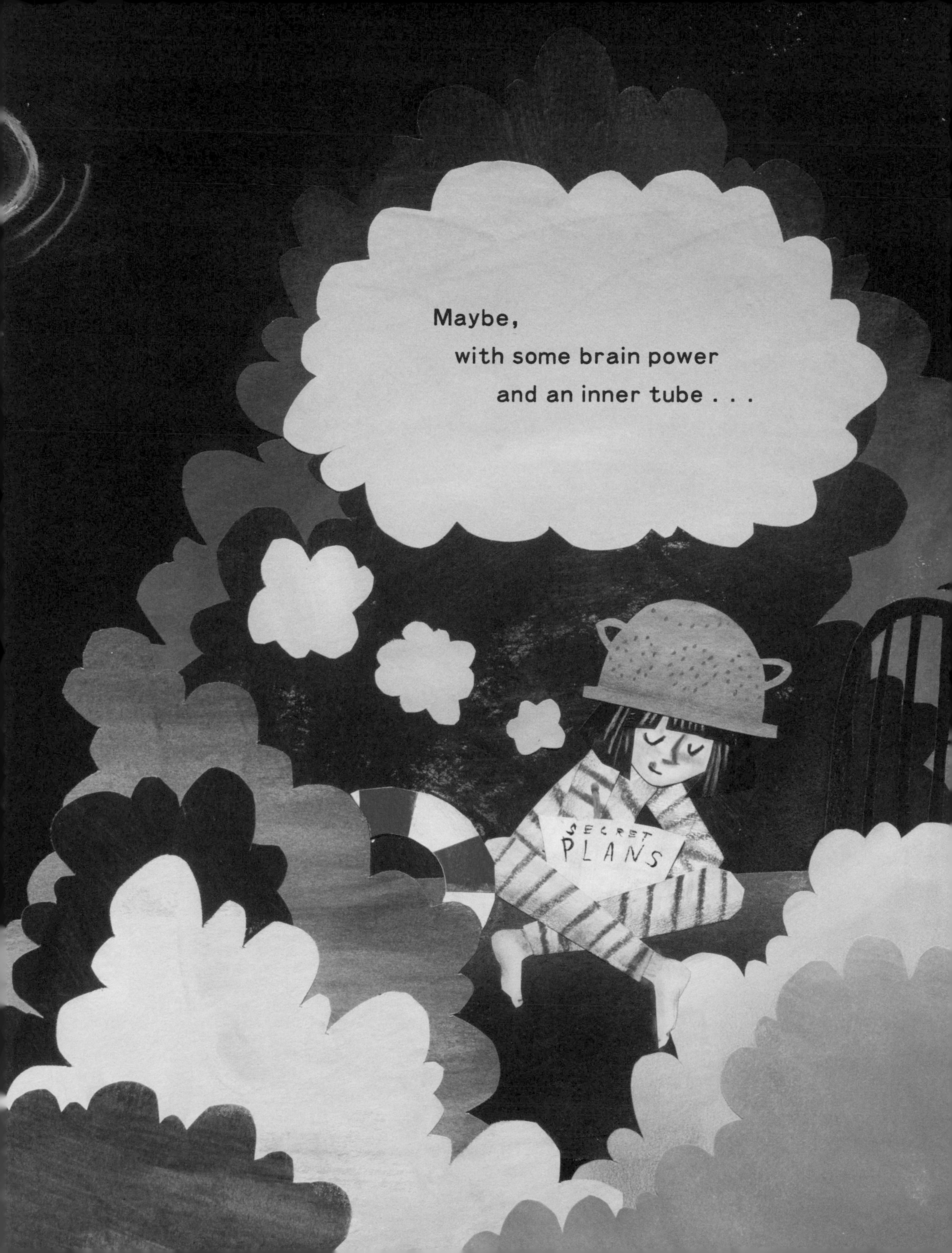

some tape and glue
and rocket juice . . .

a ladder, a crane, and a **BIG VAMOOSE**,

I'll blast that

MONSTER to the MOON!

MOON OR BUST
DANGER HAIRY SPIDER
10
9
8
7
6
5
4
THREEEEEEEK

IT MOVED!

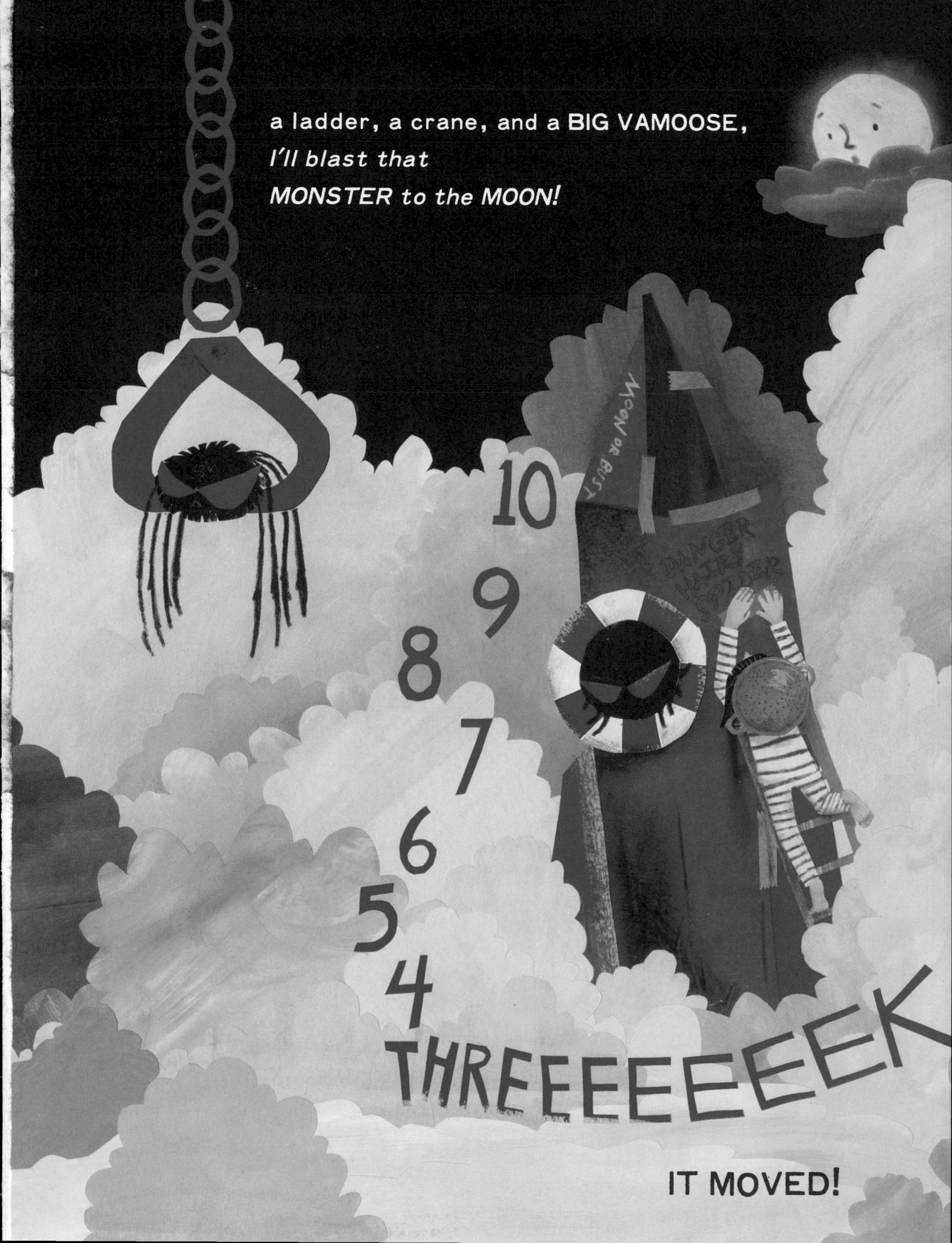

You're not huge at all. You're just . . .

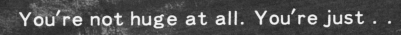

Wait a minute . . .

itsy bitsy.

Maybe YOU'RE scared of ME.

Don't worry, there's nothing
to be scared about.
I bet you'd just like to go home.

Night, Oscar.
Night, Harry.

TO RELOCATE a SURPRISE GUEST,
you will need:
A GLASS
SOME CARDBOARD
A KIND HEART
(and perhaps courage)
FIRST,
give it a
little name.
HARRY
(TAKE A
DEEEEEP
BREATH!)